Jenneli's Dance

By Elizabeth Denny

Illustrated by Chris Auchter

Theytus Books

www.theytus.com

Library and Archives Canada Cataloguing in Publication

Denny, Elizabeth, 1972-
Jenneli's dance / by Elizabeth Denny ; illustrated by Chris Auchter.

ISBN 978-1-894778-61-9

1. Métis--Juvenile fiction. I. Auchter, Chris II. Title.

PS8607.E673J45 2008   jC813'.6   C2008-903723-5

Printed in China

Mixed Sources
Product group from well-managed
forests, and other controlled sources
www.fsc.org Cert no. SGS-COC-003563
© 1996 Forest Stewardship Council
FSC

Printed on Ancient Forest Friendly 100% post consumer fibre paper.

www.theytus.com

In Canada:
Theytus Books
Green Mountain Rd., Lot 45
RR#2, Site 50, Comp. 8
Penticton, BC V2A 6J7
tel: 250-493-7181

In the USA:
Theytus Books
P.O. Box 2890
Oroville Washington
98844

Theytus Books acknowledges the support of the following:
We acknowledge the financial support of the Government of Canada
through the Book Publishing Industry Development Program
(BPIDP) for our publishing activities. We acknowledge the support
of the Canada Council for the Arts which last year invested $20.1
million in writing and publishing throughout Canada. Nous
remercions de son soutien le Conseil des Arts du Canada, qui
a investi 20,1 millions de dollars l'an dernier dans les lettres et
l'édition à travers le Canada. We acknowledge the support of the
Province of British Columbia through the British Columbia Arts
Council.

  Canada Council Conseil des Arts
for the Arts du Canada

 BRITISH COLUMBIA
ARTS COUNCIL

 Patrimoine Canadian
canadien Heritage

Jenneli's Dance

Dedicated to my Grandmother Cecile Minchin Leclerc

Jenneli Denbert was a shy girl, who felt like she was nothing special. At school, coming in last in foot races and always being the first one out in dodge ball made her feel like she wasn't good at anything. On top of that, Jenneli looked different than most of the kids in her class. She had darker hair and skin and her eyes were an unusual colour. It was as if they could not decide whether to be brown or green.

There was more that made Jenneli feel different from the other children in her class. She noticed most of the other children had bread in their lunches but she always brought bannock. She also liked fiddle music but didn't know any other children in the class who knew about fiddle music. The sound of the fiddle made her heart skip and jump and twirl. Fiddle music reminded her of Grandma Lucee.

Visiting Grandma Lucee was always a lot of fun. She lived in the country, near a town called Lakeside in Manitoba. Lakeside was away from the noise and crowds of the city, and Jenneli loved to go there. Jenneli would visit Grandma Lucee at Christmastime and would often spend weekends and summers there, as well. At Christmastime there would be lots of food and music and dancing. Jenneli's favourite song was the Red River Jig. She and all of her cousins would move their feet quickly to the music. Grandma Lucee taught Jenneli and her cousins the forward, backward and sideways steps and while they danced Grandma Lucee would shout out the changes.

Many times Grandma Lucee had told Jenneli and her cousins about the Métis fiddler from years before. This Métis fiddler had been listening to a man playing a song on an instrument called the bagpipes. The Métis man was on one side of the Red River and the bagpiper was on the other. The Métis man liked the sound of the bagpipes and started to play along. As he played, the Métis man started to make up his own song, playing the fiddle in a very fast way. Grandma Lucee said that as the man played this new song, people would dance. Because the Métis man was by the river when the song was made up, both the song and the dance became known as the Red River Jig. Grandma Lucee said that their ancestors, the Métis people, had been doing the Red River Jig for over a hundred years. Jenneli felt proud knowing that she was dancing a dance that was special to her people for so many years.

One day early in summer, while Jenneli and Grandma Lucee were having a picnic lunch, Grandma Lucee announced that there was going to be a fair at Lakeside and that she planned on taking Jenneli. Jenneli became very excited. The thought of going on the rides, eating cotton candy and candy apples made her heart skip and jump and twirl.

Grandma Lucee made another announcement. "There is going to be a jigging contest at the Fair this year... and... I entered you in it."

Jenneli was horrified and excited at the same time! It was one thing to jig in Grandma Lucee's living room but it was entirely another to jig on stage in front of a crowd!

The excitement caused Jenneli to swallow her bannock too quickly and she began to cough and sputter. Her face turned red.

"Grandma, I can't!"

Grandma Lucee jumped up from her side of the picnic table. "Can't breathe? Oh, dear, let me help y—"

"No! I mean I can't go in the contest!"

"Of course you can," Grandma Lucee said. "You jig well. And it's for kids six to ten years old, so you are just the right age!"

Jenneli's hands were shaking now at the thought of being in front of a lot of people. Her heart began to pound so hard she felt and heard it booming in her head. "I-I'm too..."

"What?"

"Shy," Jenneli said, and tears came to her eyes.

Grandma Lucee put her arm around Jenneli's shoulders. "There, there, my girl," she said. "The contest is not for another month, you have plenty of time to practise."

Grandma Lucee handed Jenneli a surprise she had hidden under the table; a new pair of shoes. "These should help."

Jenneli hugged Grandma Lucee; she loved the new shoes. She was still a little scared but she felt much better.

The following Monday, Jenneli brought her new shoes to school for show-and-tell. When it was Jenneli's turn for show-and-tell, she stood up in the front of the class with her new shoes. The kids in her class thought they were very pretty and Jenneli felt special. She told her classmates that the shoes were given to her by her Grandma Lucee and explained what the shoes were for.

A boy named Jack raised his hand, "You got shoes for JIGGING?" he smirked. Jenneli could hear a few snickers. "What do you need THOSE for? It's not like you are running a race or anything!"

The children waited to hear Jenneli's reply. Suddenly Jenneli felt silly and stammered, "I-it-it—"

The teacher, Ms. Johnson, smiled at her and spoke up. "Jigging is much harder than you think, Jack," said Ms. Johnson. Jenneli was thankful she did not have to say anything else. Ms. Johnson explained, "You have to remember a lot of steps, and hear the changes in the music, and keep time with the fiddle."

"What do you mean 'a lot of steps?'" Jack said, sneering.

I know there is no music, Jenneli, but could you show us a step?" Ms. Johnson asked.

Frightened, Jenneli showed the children her forward step, the first step she ever learned. Ms. Johnson told the class they could stand up and try to follow along if they wanted. Some of the children tried it. They teetered and stumbled and nearly fell down!

At recess time, instead of playing dodge ball, most of the children gathered around Jenneli. She helped them with their forward step until they all did it well. Even Jack could not stay away. He did not jig but he watched closely.

Jenneli felt a little bit better about her jigging by the end of that day.

The day of the fair finally came and Grandma Lucee took Jenneli all over the fair grounds. Jenneli went on the Ferris wheel and the bumper cars and the teacups. She was even able to get Grandma Lucee to walk with her in the haunted house!

When the time neared for the jigging contest, Jenneli started to feel scared again. "I'm not sure I want to go in, Grandma," Jenneli said.

"You will do just fine, Jenneli," Grandma Lucee said. "Besides, the first prize is ten dollars."

Ten dollars! Jenneli thought. That is a lot of money. She could buy more tickets, go on more rides and play as many games as she wanted with ten dollars!

Grandma Lucee squeezed Jenneli's hand. "Last chance, Jenneli, the contest starts in fifteen minutes."

"Okay," Jenneli said sharply. She said it fast so she couldn't change her mind.

Grandma Lucee and Jenneli made their way toward the outdoor stage and climbed onto the bleachers. Up on stage Jenneli could see there was a fiddler and a guitar player. The sound of them tuning their instruments made Jenneli very nervous and she began to shake. Suddenly, she realized something.

"Grandma! How will I know when to change steps?!" Her eyes were wide. "If you're way up here, you can't tell me when to change steps. Oh, Grandma! I'm going to lose!"

"Now, dear, be calm," Grandma Lucee said. "Remember what I told you before, you can hear the change in the music. If you can't, then you just watch me," she said. "I'll go like this,"—Grandma Lucee crossed and uncrossed her fingers—"when it's time to change."

Jenneli sat shaking and clutching Grandma Lucee's hand, hoping the man with the brown hair, brown skin and deep brown eyes had taken her name off the list. The first contestant was a boy about six years old. He jigged very well but only knew one change. The second contestant was a girl around ten years old who wore shiny shoes that made a neat clicking sound when she danced. Jenneli didn't even recognize the steps that she was doing and felt completely scared. There was no way she was going to beat that girl!

"Hmph!" Jenneli heard Grandma Lucee grunt. "That girl isn't jigging, she's step-dancing."

Jenneli wasn't sure she knew the difference. All she knew was that the crowd clapped very loudly when the girl was done—so loudly that Jenneli almost didn't hear the man's booming voice calling her name.

"JENNELI DENBERT."

As Jenneli made her way to the stage, her knees seemed to be knocking so hard she thought for sure the crowd could hear. As soon as the music began to play, Jenneli looked up at Grandma Lucee. What she saw made her tremble even more. Sitting right in front of Grandma Lucee was a woman wearing a large sunhat with flowers and birds on top! Jenny couldn't see Grandma Lucee's hands!

Jenneli could hear the music start to play but was frozen on the spot. Her face was burning, her legs were shaking but somehow, she started to shuffle her feet. The only thing she could see was the stage and the only thing she could hear was the music.

The music! Jenneli remembered Grandma Lucee telling her about listening for the changes in the music. She heard the fiddle melody change and she knew it was time! She shuffled her feet and hopped into her forward step. Jenneli looked down at her feet. They were moving so fast she could hardly see them. Then, Jenneli heard the fiddle melody change again and she knew it was time to change her step again.

Grandma Lucee was so proud as she watched Jenneli's feet change steps and move forward and back, and heard the new shoes slide across the floor in a clean swoop followed by a hard tap.

Before the song was over, Jenneli had time to do her backward and crossways steps. At last the music started to slow down. When the music finally stopped Jenneli was totally out of breath. The crowd applauded loudly. Jenneli's face was warm, her heart was beating fast and her feet felt really hot. She was so happy that the hardest part was over and so excited that she'd finally learned to hear the changes in the music that she hardly even watched the very last dancer.

Then it came time to hear the winners.

In third place was the dancer that had jigged right after Jenneli. In second place was the girl with the clickity shoes. In first place, was Jenneli!

The man with the brown hair, brown skin and deep brown eyes shook her hand and said. "Not many young children can do three changes of the Red River Jig, Jenneli. Congratulations!" Along with the prize money, to Jenneli's surprise, he handed her a shining trophy. Holding the prize money and her trophy made her heart skip and jump and twirl.

When Jenneli walked back to the bleachers, she got a big squeeze and a kiss on the forehead from Grandma Lucee. "I knew you could do it!" Grandma Lucee said.

Hand in hand they walked back towards the rides and games.

"I'm proud of you," Grandma Lucee said, and squeezed Jenneli's hand.

"Thank you for putting me in the contest," Jenneli said.

"Thank you for staying in the contest," Grandma Lucee said and smiled. "You can take that trophy to school for show-and-tell."

It was a good day. Jenneli won first place in her first jigging contest. She had heard the changes in the music for the very first time and for the very first time she knew she was good at something.

When Jenneli went back to school, she felt that being different was a very good thing indeed. Being Métis made her feel like there was something special about her after all.

ABOUT THE RED RIVER JIG

THE RED RIVER JIG has become somewhat of an anthem of the Métis people since its birth in the Red River Settlement (Manitoba) over one and a half centuries ago. Although there is more than one legend surrounding its composition, the story of the Métis fiddler imitating Scottish bagpipes he heard from across the river is one of the most common and most popular stories of the jig's origin.

There are numerous written accounts by both Métis and non-Métis people having witnessed the Red River Jig throughout the nineteenth century, where it seemed to garner the most popularity among the Métis people. Métis people are noted for their precision with respect to the dance, with some of the fiercest competitors developing their own original changes—which makes it nearly impossible to know just how many steps of the Red River Jig currently exist. Even today, the Red River Jig is part and parcel of most Métis celebrations across the Nation.